An
Anglo-Indian
in Love

Tapan Ghosh

First published in 2018 by

Becomeshakespeare.com

Wordit Content Design & Editing Services Pvt Ltd
Unit - 26, Building A -1, Nr Wadala RTO,
Wadala (East), Mumbai 400037, India
T: +91 8080226699

Wordit Art Fund helps deserving authors publish
their work by providing monetary support.
To apply for funding, please visit us at
www.BecomeShakespeare.com

Cover designed by Tapan Ghosh

This book is a work of fiction. Names, characters, places, and
incidents either are products of the author's imagination or are
used fictitiously. Any resemblance to actual persons, living or dead,
events, or locales is entirely coincidental.

Tapan Ghosh
Visit my website at www.tapanghosh.com

ISBN- 978-93-88573-00-9

Foreword

It is said that the memories of one's growing years form the deepest impressions. Nothing could be truer. In the mid-1950s I spent my early years in Calcutta when the city's culture was a blend of the colonial times and the first flush of independence. It was an interesting mix which made Calcutta one of the most livable cities in the country. Optimism and hope mingled with old world charm to offer the denizen the best of both worlds.

As a 10-year old student of the Our Lady Queen of the Mission School referred to in this story, the Anglo-Indians made a big impact on me. Especially the flamboyant sort who rode powerful motorcycles with sexy girls in short skirts riding pillion. As I grew older, this community dwindled in number, as many of them migrated to the UK, Australia, Canada and other places around the world.

This community was born out of the union of British men and women of Indian origin in early colonial times. This union was encouraged by the rulers to expand their presence significantly. It created for them a workforce for top positions in the railways, missionary schools, customs, excise, posts & telegraph and forest departments and elsewhere. Their control was complete and the Anglo-Indians were more British in their ways than the British themselves.

This story is about a married Anglo-Indian who falls in love with an Indian boy young enough to be her son. The story also refers to the deep-rooted scar of the white-skin complex left by the Anglo-Indian community which continues to exist to this day. Though a piece of fiction, the story draws heavily from incidents I was witness to during my growing years.

I hope that I have been successful in my attempt. For this story is my tribute to the city I cherish. A place of which I have the fondest of memories. Strange as it may sound, I haven't had the opportunity to visit it ever since I left it half-a-century ago. I hope both, the city and I, won't be separated for much longer anymore.

Tapan Ghosh

1. THE FOOTBALL MATCH

Football matches at the Park Circus maidaan are a common sight. The ground has six pitches, most of them occupied during summer evenings by local teams made up of college-going players. Passers-by tend to linger a while, expressing support for one team or another. Those keen to follow a full game squat on the grass around the periphery of the pitch, inching into the playing area as the game progresses. They are so close to the action that they are almost a part of it. It's like watching a play where your seat is adjacent to and on the same level as the stage. However, unlike in a theatre, you have to be alert at all times, lest a ball hit you.

That evening was no different. The Anglo-Indian Park Union team was playing in red jerseys and the Desh Bandhoos in blue. All attention seemed to be riveted on them. Other teams, playing without proper uniforms, came across as ragged outfits in comparison. Most of the spectators being Bengali-speaking, were Desh Bandhoo supporters. This cheered the team no end. An unusual sight that evening was the presence of a sizeable number of enthusiastic Anglo-Indian girls among the spectators.

Desh Bandhoo were being ably led by Dilip dada (elder brother), as he was called. Eighteen-year old Dilip was a big brother indeed. A hooligan and a bully, everyone feared him. As the whistle blew, he took control of the ball. Playing centre-forward with nimble footwork, he dribbled well. Moving skillfully through his opponents, he was in possession of the ball for almost a minute before passing it to his left-in, who managed to take control after some hic-ups. The left-in was a fast runner; he took charge and move towards the D. The opponents offered good resistance as they seemed to be a better team. Dilip was desperately waiting for a pass but it was almost a lost cause by the time he got one. It took a huge effort from him to dive to a header to score that goal. The crowd erupted into cries of *"dada, dada."*

THE FIRST LOOK

An Anglo-Indian woman gave Dilip a beaming smile. "What a beauty!" thought Dilip, as their eyes met. A youngish-looking girl whispered something in her ears. He recalled the girl standing near their goal post with her friends, while the Desh Bandhoo players were changing for the match. Being a make-shift football pitch, there were no changing rooms on the ground. The players hadn't taken kindly to this intrusion and Dilip, who was being scrutinised by the girls, had done something drastic. As if by accident, he had pulled down his football shorts to reveal something that had them scandalised. They had shot off immediately, much to the amusement of Dilip's team mates who had had a hearty laugh, *(dada, hat's off to you)*"

The tables turned on Desh Bandhoo as the game progressed. Park Union were now able to penetrate their defense and score without much effort. The Anglo-Indian girls were proving to be a great distraction in their miniskirts, playing cheer leaders every time Park Union scored a goal. The leg show and the lusty cries of the spectators ensured that Dilip and his mates could hardly concentrate on their game. It appeared to be a losing cause.

What happened next was not in the spirit of the game. A major dispute broke out as the referee wrongly called an offside. Supporters from either side invaded the pitch and beat up the referee before attacking the players. The game had degenerated into a fight between the two sides and their supporters. Given the sheer number of supporters, Desh Bandhoos held the upper hand. The situation was indeed grave for the Anglo-Indian women; their safety was in question. Sensing the danger, Dilip headed in the direction of Cindy, the Anglo-Indian woman who had smiled at him, placed her on his broad shoulders and ran to the safety of a building across the road. The wail of police sirens drowned out her screams.

OPERATION RESCUE

Dilip rushed to a balcony on the first floor of the building. He put Cindy down, but held on to her hand in a firm grip, only to be stung by a tight slap across his left cheek. This shook him up. He was about to retaliate when she screamed,

"You want to rape me, you scoundrel. Why have you brought me here?" Dilip did not know what to say, he just tried to calm her down but she wriggled out of his grip. He was mesmerised by her looks and started to move towards her. "Stay away from me," she screamed and he stopped dead. She is a strong woman, he thought. "I am sorry," he said. Composing herself, she looked down at the scene below and exclaimed, "Oh my God!"

By now the police had assumed control and were busy rounding up the rioters and the girls. Dilip saw her concern. He wanted to calm her down, but equally, he was aching to take her in his arms. "Don't you dare touch me," she exploded like a lioness, "I am old enough to be your mother." He was aghast in disbelief. He noticed her looking at the girls who were handcuffed and being led to the police van. She looked at Dilip sternly and again looked at the scene below in helplessness. "I am their teacher and look what I have done," she said and broke down. Dilip was shaken up. He was dying to make amends and struggling to think of a way to help her out of this mess. "It's not wise for me to go down now, they will arrest me too. How will that help?" she asked. "I will do, whatever you, you..." Dilip started to stammer, his desire to be in her arms grew ten-fold. Dilip saw her look of disgust as she told him, "You have such a dirty mind, you deliberately undressed in front of my students."

"I am sorry, I didn't mean to, it was just a reflex action in the heat of the moment. I will do whatever you say now," said Dilip. "Let's go the police station to bail them out," she commanded. Dilip sprang into action. He ran down and she after him. He hailed a rickshaw. The last vestige of colonial rule in India, the rickshaw was the most common mode of transport in Calcutta. Cindy's and Dada's minds were racing as the rickshaw sped to the police station. The vehicle had its destination cut out; the passengers were unsure of their own.

A FLOOD OF MEMORIES

Cindy glared at the boy beside her in the rickshaw. Too shy to look directly at her, she knew that he had been trying to steal glimpses of her from time to time. He appeared to be a sensitive lad from a decent background but a victim of dysfunctional upbringing. She looked at his innocent baby face and big eyes. Suddenly, she began to see him as her own son, a three-month old infant, suckling her breast. She quickly turned her head away to conceal her feelings. She was shocked, she couldn't understand; her son had died 18 years ago. She was so young at that time that it had taken her several years to overcome the trauma. This lad had brought back those sad memories. She was having a tough time keeping her eye off Dilip. She felt like taking him in her arms and then again she was horrified at the thought. She was confused. How could she associate someone like Dilip – a ruffian and rapist – with her dead son? Life can be so confusing, she thought, but always with a reason.

CINDY, THE ANGLO-INDIAN

Dilip would settle his gaze on Cindy whenever he found her immersed in her thoughts. He would look down immediately whenever he found her looking at him. *Oee lojjaye matha ta jhukiye raakhto.* (he put his head down in shame). He found her very young and attractive and wondered how she could be of his mother's age. For that matter she appeared to have the wisdom and maturity of his mother.

However, Cindy was an emotional wreck. An Anglo-Indian, 36 years of age with a lovely skin, she was the result of a handsome young captain's affair with a beautiful Indian girl. The girl's parents were helpless. The couple were truly in love and Cindy was a love child, a perfect cross between the two. The colonial rulers had made these marriages illegal towards the end of their stay in India, despite encouraging such unions at the onset of colonial power, as it had helped them establish their presence in the country.

Cindy was a brilliant teacher of English literature and a very popular model. Her sexy body and sizzling walk were irresistible. She was a passionate lover and had been through some torrid affairs, both, before and after her first marriage. She loved her husband and they got along well. He was a nice man but a born loser. Not being smart enough to make money, the onus of being the breadwinner fell upon Cindy. He then took to drinking. She did everything to get him out of the habit, but in vain. He died of cirrhosis of the liver. Cindy was heartbroken.

Cindy had subsequently had an affair and with a colleague, an Anglo-Indian Physical Training (PT) teacher, a big-built man with the physique of an athlete. The pair was the talk of the town and they eventually married with the entire school attending the wedding. Relations soured soon as Bert - her husband - turned out to be a selfish man. He was beastly by nature while she was a giver and did everything possible to keep him happy. He considered that as his birthright and gave back nothing in return. Inconsiderate to the core, he would spend all his money on himself, not sparing a word of appreciation for the woman who served him lovingly in bed and elsewhere. This depressed Cindy no end, especially since Bert least cared about keeping his infidelities under wraps from their social group.

A HAPPY ENDING

Dilip was now concentrating on getting the lot out of police custody. This wasn't easy. His prayers were answered when someone called out his name. "Dilip, *kothai jachees, memer shonge. (Dilip, where are you going with madam?)*." This man was his godfather and a powerful one at that. Dilip was so thrilled that he jumped down from the running rickshaw to talk to the man in the gleaming Morris Minor.

To cut a long story short, it ended well for those interned at the police station. All the footballers and supporters - some with bandages and others with exposed wounds - were released with a simple warning. Dilip was glad to see that none of the girls were injured. The crowd broke into an applause, *"dada, dada"* again. For the first time Dilip chided them. Something in him had changed. He had sobered down a lot following the encounter with Cindy. "Thank you, Dilip, my name is Cindy," she said, extending her hand. Dilip was dazed as he politely shook hands before Cindy went off with her students.

2. A GLIMPSE INTO THE PAST

DILIP, THE DADA

Dilip stood there for a long time, thinking about Cindy and the Anglo-Indian community. He remembered an incident that had recently taken place at Park Circus. The Our Lady Queen of the Missions convent school close by was for girls, with boys being permitted only till class V. Older boys from neighbouring schools such as St. Xavier's and La Martiniere used to frequent this place to flirt with the lovely Anglo-Indian girls there.

The Anglo-Indian boys on Indian Chiefs had pretty girls in skirts riding pillion and showing off their legs. This was a common sight in the Park Circus and the Park Street areas of central Calcutta. The school kids would see them during the lunch break when they could peek outside the gate, feasting on their one anna worth of mutton patties, pastry, cream roll or Magnolia ice cream stick bought from the hawkers who were allowed to sell inside the school compound. The older girls would sneak out on some pretext and be with the rowdy rich boys on motorcycles. The boys would come back again at school-closing time. That was the only time the younger boys, who were envious of the outsiders, mustered the courage to get their kicks out of pushing aside the older boys and pretty girls.

A ten-year-old boy named Haresh had to pay for this. One day he was cornered by three big boys on motorcycles. They threatened to run him over. Terrified, the kid ran to the nearest building. The bikers followed and pinned him down. He was up against the wall, horrified by the growling of the old army bikes and pleading for mercy. Just then, he heard a loud authoritative voice calling out to him, "Horesh, Horesh."

"Dada," answered Haresh as his face brightened up. The bikers turned back, quite shaken as they looked at Dada's smiling face. Their engines went dead. Dada had quite a reputation. A law unto himself, he had the knack of being at the right place at the right time.

Worshipped by some and dreaded by others, he once picked up a groom from the wedding mandap (*arena*), replaced him with the bride's lover and worked the ceremony through. There was a pin drop silence all around, Dada's gang ensured that no one left the premises while the ceremony was in progress.

Dada and Haresh were residents of Mushtaq Mahal building and good friends. Being eight years older than Haresh, Dada was protective towards his friend. "Is this the best you have here?" he enquired, glaring at the boys and pointing to the one on the red bike. The boys were too scared to speak. They didn't know what was coming next. Dada picked up the boy on the red bike, lifted him high and threw him towards the other two, bringing all of them down with their bikes. All in one go! *"Horesh, esho, bosho ekhane, (come, come, sit down here)"* said Dada, pointing to the rear seat of the red bike before driving off with the jubilant kid.

LOCATING CINDY

Dilip's thoughts were now with the Anglo-Indians and how they must hate his guts. But with Cindy turning out to be from the community, he bore no animosity towards them. He often recalled the handshake with Cindy. *Bilkul lattoo ho gaya tha, saala* (he was completely enamoured of her). What he could not see at that time was the affection for him in Cindy's eyes. All he wanted to do now was to get her address and woo her. Given his connections, the address wasn't difficult to obtain. He set off for Buckingham Court, 113B Ripon Street, off Park Street to see her residence. It was a two-storied circular structure with a football ground-size inner courtyard.

This was one of several European-style buildings the British built for the middle class. The profusion of such buildings in Neo-Gothic, Baroque and Neoclassical styles they built is testimony to Calcutta being the second-best city in the British Empire after London during the colonial era of 1700-1912 when it was the capital of British India. Dilip went there twice in quick succession but was careful not to be seen. He was not lucky though to spot her on either occasion.

A MARRIAGE GONE SOUR

Had Dilip witnessed the scene inside her apartment, he would not have tolerated it. Bert was physically abusive and though shivering with rage, Cindy was no match for his strength. He kept pushing her till she fell on the bed. "Just leave me alone, I'll give you two tight raps," she exploded.

"You'll give? Ha, I'll give you one jhaap (*slap*), you'll go flying, you know where? Up there, where your first husband is."

"Don't you dare talk about him, he was such an angel," shot back Cindy, crying.

"Angel! Shaala, such a bloody boozard! Angel? *Kookoorer baachha shaala. (you son of a dog, bastard)*"

Cindy ran out of the room boiling with anger, banging the door behind her. "You have no business to be here, I'm going to throw you out of my house." Once the envy of the entire community, this is what the marriage had come to.

THE PLIGHT OF THE ANGLO-INDIANS

It was not easy for an Anglo-Indian to survive in the country, post-independence. They were shunned by the Indians who called them *chi chi*; a derogatory term. They were accepted as equals, neither by the British, nor by the Indians. They, however, considered themselves British, adopted the customs of the rulers and were more British in their ways than the British themselves. They were loyal to the British Raj and worked diligently for it. The backbone of the British, they ran the police force, railways and schools. They were also divided, as the ones who were more British in their appearance and characteristics were given preference. As a result, they had higher status and better jobs. On the other hand, the ones with more Indian looks had better rapport with the Indians.

This race was caught between the devil and the deep sea. They were like the washer man's dog: *dhobi ka kutta, na ghar ka na ghat ka* (they were neither here nor there). The Indians were not responsible for their lowly social position. Rather, it was the British whose own morals were so low that they had no qualms about leaving their progeny in the lurch. The community blended the richness of Indian culture with the progressive thinking of the British. Besides, they were blessed with attractive physical features.

3. CHANGING EQUATIONS

MAKING MOVES AT THE CONCERT

Dilip was dying to see Cindy, his God-sent angel. He did get lucky when he attended a concert, courtesy Liora David and family, one of the Jew families settled in Calcutta. Liora, his childhood friend, was tall and pretty-looking and from his Park Circus neighbourhood. She had always had the hots for Dilip, but Dilip hadn't given any serious thought to their relationship.

This concert was a hit with the Cavaliers stealing the show. Dilip looked out of place despite being in an outfit especially selected by Liora. He got a start when he saw Cindy on the floor doing the Latin hustle, the latest variation of Rock 'n' Roll. Harry Webb, the lead singer, was going gaga over the way she danced to his music. Now it was Liora's turn to get a jolt when she saw the mesmerising effect Cindy had on Dilip.

Liora forced Dilip to get on the floor but Dilip's moves were quite awkward as this culture was alien to him. Though an elegant dancer, Liora did not impress Dilip. *Ghar ki murgi dal barabar!* (familiarity breeds contempt). The place was packed and Dilip ensured that Cindy did not notice him. Towards the end however, Cindy came across Dilip and Liora. Dilip noticed the enquiring look on her face before she was pulled away by her group. This brief encounter had a calming effect on Dilip.

ADOPTING A NEW CULTURE

After the show Dilip decided to work on his dancing skills. He quickly cultivated some Anglo-Indian lads and decided to adopt their culture. He spent hours listening to Rock music played by the legendary Radio Ceylon broadcaster, Vernon Corea on Binaca Hit Parade. Dean Martin, Frank Sinatra and Bobby Darin were favourites but and

Elvis Presley was above them all. He would often go to parties with his newly-acquired friends and dance there. Most people dared not ignore him because of his reputation as a dada and the fact that he was well-connected. Sometimes, he would go over to meet Liora and display his newly-acquired dancing skills. She had a gramophone on which she played records and Dilip would sing and dance with her. She partnered him whenever he wanted. He reciprocated the gesture by taking her out for movies and meals. Liora was longing for some intimacy but Dilip was in a world of his own, the look on his face suggested that he belonged to a much more mature generation. He learnt to sing too, as he had a naturally good and powerful voice.

LIORA, THE FRIEND FROM CHILDHOOD

Born a sickly child, Liora was two years younger to Dilip who always considered her a baby. She had grown up admiring him and there was no question of any other boy in her life. A skinny, lanky and awkward-looking child, she was now tall, strong and pretty, thanks to Dilip who had encouraged her to play a variety of sport. Both Dilip and Liora used to look at themselves in a long mirror at her place and admire the drastic changes that had taken place gradually over the past four years. Being smart and mentally strong, she would often get physical with Dilip, using her weight and all her strength to pin him down. This happened again when Dilip turned up for dance practice with her. He missed a step and fell on the jute carpet and she over him. This time she held on to him tightly. He pretended to struggle and her cheeks flushed in enjoyment. This was so irresistible that he ended up kissing her cheek. He did not want to take advantage of the proximity because he loved her in another way. He was not a saint, but now it was only Cindy. Liora was wise enough to realise that Dilip, who was so caring and protective otherwise, did not love her in the same way. This made her extremely sad but she was mature enough not to express it. Her love was causeless, she just wanted to see Dilip happy. Sensing that Dilip would not go beyond the peck on the cheek, she got up and brought cakes and a bottle of lemonade to pamper him. She switched on the Radiogram and both started to sing along.

One and a two and I love you, I love you, I love you

I hope that you love me too, let's play the game of love

Three and a four, couldn't want you more, want you more, want you more

A hug and a kiss and I knew for sure, let's play the game of love

That's how it goes in the books I've read where the rules are written down

When a boy meets a girl, not a word is said but the heart goes round and round

THE FIGHT AT CINDY'S PLACE

Dilip went to Cindy's house again a few days later, this time at night when Cindy was likely to be home. Besides, he could get closer to the apartment unnoticed. Standing outside a window, he heard Cindy's voice.

Then he got a shock on hearing a man shouting at her. Cindy began to cry. Dilip was concerned and he rang the doorbell. Bert opened the door and

Dilip noticed that the situation inside was far from cordial. Bert had a look of disgust on his face. He glared at Dilip, shouting, *"Kone he eddar que aaya? (Who are you? Why are you here?)"* in Anglo-Hindi, a hybrid used only to speak with Indian servants. Dilip had never been spoken to like this before. He reacted by raising his finger at Bert. Bert screamed, *"Get out, you kaala aadmi (darkie)".* Dilip lost all control; this was the biggest insult to an Indian by a white-skin. In his rage he grabbed Bert by the collar. This was quite a sight as Bert, a hulk, much bigger than Dilip had never been held like that by a dark brown Indian. He battered Dilip while Cindy screamed, "Don't! Please don't beat him, please," and tried to pull Bert away. Bert smacked her face and threw her flat on the ground. This was more than what Dilip could take.

Jumping up with all his energy, he landed flying kicks and headers on Bert. Dilip was in his element and the football was Bert's round head. There was nothing stopping Dilip now and what's more, Cindy applauded him but she stopped him before he totally slaughtered Bert.

Now what! Cindy and Dilip looked at each other, concerned about the other's bruises. Bert was forgotten till he stirred a bit. Cindy's and Dilip's problems were far from over, in fact they had just started. Bert had to be hospitalised. The matter was not reported to the police. The hospital was told that he had slipped down a staircase and injured himself.

HEADING TOWARDS ANOTHER CONFRONTATION

Bert was discharged from the hospital with bandages on his head and face, arousing sympathy and concern amongst a section of Anglo-Indians who were more British than the rest. They were extremely hostile and wanted revenge, the others didn't. They were wise enough not to take on Dilip dada and gang.

Dada was in no position to avoid this confrontation either. His followers wanted to avenge the insult to their dada. Dilip couldn't get Cindy out of his mind. He was only concerned about Cindy's opinion of him. Did she think of him as a downright hooligan? He was certainly at fault for going to her place uninvited but she was trying to protect him. He was a changed man now. He had outgrown the sense of importance he felt about being pampered by the politicians who used him to win elections.

Things between Bert and Cindy worsened. Bert started showing his true colours as he recovered; he was constantly surrounded by his sycophants. The rift between Cindy and Bert came out in the open and caused an upheaval amongst the Anglo-Indians. There were now two distinct groups, the out and out conformists were on Bert's side and the rest on Cindy's and Dilip's side. The ones with Dilip considered him a local hero who had helped many people, like at the police station after the football fiasco. Besides, he had recently befriended many of them.

The match would be like a game of hockey, but it would be fought, not played. There would be hockey sticks but no ball! No goal posts! There would be no extras, only eleven a side. The number would gradually reduce to maybe even none. Many stretchers were lined up for the face off. To avoid police interference, the confrontation would take place in the inner courtyard of Cindy's residential block where she had two apartments. The one on the ground floor where she presently lived with Bert had belonged to her late husband. The other - a one-bedroom with a large hall on the first floor - had been bought from her own earnings. She planned to use it as a dancing school.

The general feeling was tense since the match was uppermost on everyone's mind. The teams would meet every evening after work, practicing their swings, egged on by their supporters. Bert was totally fit and he used to come for vigorous practice sessions. Dilip was more involved in building his team. Surprisingly, Dilip's team had a good number of Anglo-Indian supporters. He also had eight Anglo-Indians in his team, especially selected by him on the basis of built, dodging power and swing power. Anglo-Indians had always been good at hockey, having been a part of India's gold winning campaigns at the Olympics, winning six golds in a row.

A HORRIFIC INCIDENT

There were only six days left for D-day when a horrific incident took place. An Indian stepped on the foot of an Englishman from the Deputy High Commission who happened to be traveling by tram. The foreigner pushed him aside and called out, "*Kala aadmi, damn fool.*" Everyone in the tram exploded with anger. There were riots all over Calcutta with trams and vehicles being set on fire. The city was paralysed. Night curfew was imposed. Politicians were active and Dilip dada was at their beck and call.

As the city moved towards normalcy, there was a sigh of relief, especially amongst the Anglo-Indians. They were called *kutcha butcha* by the locals. It was a derogatory term, meaning '*half-baked*'. The lighter-skinned Anglo-Indians like Bert were more insecure and more inclined to migrate and they did just that.

Bert, who was eagerly waiting for normalcy, resumed his practice with renewed vigour. Dilip dada was nowhere to be seen. He was missing from the day of the incident, as though consumed by it. There was no sign of Dilip and people assumed that he had chickened out. There was all-round disappointment, except for Cindy who was relieved.

4. WAR AND PEACE

THE BIG FIGHT

The big day arrived. Ten minutes before the time set for the match, Dilip dada and his team arrived at the courtyard and began to practice their swings. Bert came out of his house with his team a few minutes later. Dilip kept looking at Cindy from the corner of his eyes. She looked nervous and her gaze was fixed on Dilip all the time. Dilip felt that she was trying to say something and he nodded in acknowledgement.

Just a minute before the start of the match, he addressed the entire Anglo-Indian community. He said, "The match is going to begin now. What will be the outcome? Most of the Anglo-Indians will die or be severely injured. Is that what you want? I don't think so. This is just a clash between Bert and me. I don't want you to suffer for it."

The sigh of relief could be felt by all. Some said that Dilip had chickened out. Bert exploded, "Have we wasted so much time for you to chicken out in the end. How dare you do that, we will not allow you, we have a full house for the games to begin." He sounded like the Emperor of Rome at the Coliseum.

"Let's do it right now," replied Dilip in a calm and mature tone. He said, 'The times are sensitive after the ghastly incident the other day. I was dragged into it, so I know it will not be possible to avoid the police, especially when there are mortalities. I don't think the community can take that kind of risk." He continued, "However I don't want the audience to be disappointed. I suggest that the match be played between Bert and me alone to reduce the number of deaths to only one."

There was a pin drop silence. Cindy looked shocked; she was dying to intervene and stop this nonsense. She could not bear to see Dilip hurt in anyway. "He will die only over my dead body," she said under her breath. She felt helpless; an Anglo-Indian woman couldn't be seen favouring an Indian against her Anglo-Indian husband. She almost collapsed as the confrontation between Dilip and Bert began. It looked to be one-sided as Bert had a very powerful swing and a big built to leverage his massive strength. Dilip was more graceful with dodging and had a very rhythmic swing, but otherwise he no match for Bert. Bert looked like a guy possessed and was all out for Dilip's blood. Somehow, almost the entire audience was sympathetic towards Dilip as this looked to be a very unfair fight.

Suddenly, there was a big sound of Bert's hockey stick clashing with Dilip's. The impact was so powerful that it completely shook Dilip. Cindy was badly shaken up too. Then immediately came another bang, this time it was Dilip's back being crushed by a big blow. Cindy's screech was drowned by the collective screech of the audience.

Bert was ready to finish off Dilip with a blow on his head while Dilip was lying on the ground looking completely dead. Everyone's heart was in their mouths, praying for a miracle. As Cindy came running to guard Dilip against the finishing blow from Bert's hockey stick, Dilip swiftly moved his head out of the way to see the toe of hockey stick head dig into the ground till the heal.

Dilip quickly came forward on his fours and with his hockey stick he pulled at Bert's left leg. Bert tripped and his heavy body fell on his back with a heavy thud. He was finished. Dilip quickly jumped on his chest and raised his stick up in the air to bring it down on Bert's skull. But he stopped in mid-air and said aloud, "I am stopping this nonsense. I am not a barbarian. I spare you." Saying so, he quickly went off and the rest of his team took over. The crowd rose in joy, chanting, "dada, dada."

Cindy went after Dilip and caught hold of him before he dropped to the ground. Her tears on Dilip's face brought him back to consciousness. He smiled at her before losing consciousness again. Cindy was relieved that Dilip went all out to protect Bert, entertain the audience and gain her trust, all in one go, but at the cost of risking his life.

Later, she took some stern steps in retaliation. She left Bert in her house with his friends, with a notice to vacate at once. She set up her one-bedroom apartment that she always wanted to occupy. She converted the spacious hall into a dance school and lived in the bedroom till Bert vacated her two-bedroom house. Her dancing classes were in great demand. This helped her retain her sanity while Dilip was recouping in the hospital. She kept Dilip abreast of all developments and enrolled him for dancing lessons. Dilip joined the day he was discharged from the hospital.

DADA'S TRAUMATIC CHILDHOOD

Dilip was only five years old when he was beaten up by his father. His stepmother, much younger than his father, had him totally in her grip. One day she screamed at Dilip while breastfeeding his infant brother and accused him of touching her breast. She ordered her husband to teach Dilip a lesson.

The poor child wondered why he was slapped so hard. He was shocked to know that he had done something wrong. He loved his stepmother a lot; he had never seen his biological mother as she had died during childbirth. After that day he was terrified but his desires grew strongly. He secretly watched his tiny brother possess the most precious toy. He was envious and was dying to be in his place. He used to dream of his mother loving him the same way. He wanted to draw her attention and have her cuddle him close to her breast. This never happened and he remained deprived of the mother's touch that he craved. Things had been different before his stepbrother was born; his stepmother had been quite a loving person.

It was painful for him to learn in later years that he was a step child. He detested his father all the more when he came to know that his mother had died due to gross negligence on his father's part. Thereafter, he constantly got into trouble with his father and hated him. He grew up to be a rebel. However, he was an exceptionally intelligent child, naturally good at his studies, brilliant in sports and a born leader. Unfortunately, his aggressive nature and give-a-damn attitude was cleverly exploited by the local politicians. This helped him extract all the clout and power he needed to satisfy his whims. At the young age of 18 he was a law unto himself, a feared gangster.

However, the mother fixation was something that he had to live with. No amount of exposure to the opposite sex fixed this problem. It would hurt and anger him when people ridiculed him with the taunt, "*Maine apni maa ka doodh piya hai. (I have been breast-fed by my mother)*" It would bring back the pain of his childhood, the deprivation and the sense of not being loved and cared for within his own family. At such moments he would feel that his physical strength and the influence he had over others were of little value in the absence of maternal love.

SOME EXTRA-CURRICULAR ACTIVITIES

An unusual incident took place one evening after Dilip joined Cindy's dance class. Dilip would look at her breasts which would always swell up when she danced with him. Every night she would imagine herself feeding Dilip and would end up caressing and squeezing her areolas. That day she just couldn't resist anymore. Pure love for the boy swelled up. Something in his pleading eyes did not allow her to ignore his look. She pulled him closer and dragged him to bed. She had been itching to this for a long time. She felt his mouth on her cleavage. "Oh my God, this is killing me," she gasped. She was totally helpless and one thing led to another as her nipples quivered for his lips. They were longing for them, wanting to explode as the right nipple was enclosed, urging Dilip to penetrate deeper till her entire right breast was in his mouth. "Oh God," the feel of his tongue and teeth drove her crazy as he sucked vigorously. This went on, oblivious of time. It was just bliss. It was the right breast first, then the left, and the right again. Dilip did not know what he was doing. As if by instinct, he was vigorously massaging away with his mouth and squeezing with his hands, not realising that he was in fact inducing lactation.

Cindy was imagining herself as a breastfeeding mother and Dilip, a baby that was craving for the succulent nectar from Mother Nature. Cindy suddenly made some sounds as she experienced a huge climax. Dilip followed suit as the warm nectar ejaculated in his mouth and swept down his throat. It was heavenly!

Both were lying alongside, starring at the ceiling and breathing heavily, then looking at each other. It seemed as if they did not care about the consequences. She could not resist his hands from caressing her face and when she pulled him to her lips and in no time they were entangled. Every part of his was longing for every part of hers. When he entered her, she moaned with ecstasy never experienced before; it was like her love awaiting the intruder.

MOMENTS OF INTROSPECTION

That night when Cindy was alone in bed, she was confused about what had happened between her and Dilip. What kind of love was this? Her son would have been exactly Dilip's age and how could she take him as a lover? She had no answers, this was beyond her. She could not sleep all night, she felt so guilty. Was she running Dilip's life? He was young and capable with a nice-looking girlfriend she had met the other day. Her mind was racing. Was he serious about her? Was she going to leave him? She realised that she could not do without Dilip now. He had almost killed himself to get to her. How would their communities accept this relationship? Would Jesus pardon her?

Cindy was a mess. She wanted to think right but her mind was clouded. The truth was difficult to accept but she had to get to it. She decided to seek counsel from her aunt Gloria, a woman of great wisdom and highly respected in the Anglo-Indian community.

5. CAUSELESS LOVE

DISCOVERING THE TRUTH

Next day she took a tram to Mandeville Gardens in Ballygunge opposite an upcoming public school known for its modern ways of teaching. It was located on a huge plot of land bought by Mr. Guha, the principal of the school, from Gloria. Her rich aunt was all set to receive her favourite niece today. "My, my, look at you, looking as young as ever, you don't age at all." said her dignified-looking aunt.

They hugged as if there was no tomorrow and sat down to have tea. The table was set with a teapot covered with a tea cosy, two cups and saucers of expensive bone china. Cindy was thrilled to see the apple pie Aunt Gloria was famous for. She blew a kiss to her.

Cindy told her aunt everything honestly without holding back. Her aunt, who looked shocked and objected to most of the things she said, later settled down after Cindy threatened to go away. She heard her out patiently and studied the situation. She then locked herself in the study and left Cindy pacing up and down the hallway.

Hearing her aunt on the telephone, she went to stand by the study door. "DSP sahib, how are you...thank you, any time...I'll always be available, now I have something to ask you about Dilip Paul, Dilip dada...are you saying Dilip is well connected and liked by everyone? Okay, I see. Tell me if he has any criminal record...no criminal record? How can you say that? He is a dada, not a saint...okay, Robin Hood... ha ha, Robin Hood of our generation...if you say so...okay, everyone is of that opinion...okay thank you...call you when I have something more to ask. Bye."

Cindy quickly moved away, suppressing a broad smile. Her aunt came out of the study and told Cindy that she wanted to meet Dilip. Cindy looked at her aunt, trying to gauge her.

"Why do you want to meet him?"

"Don't you want me to? You've already had two relationships that did not work. I had told you about Bert, the big hulk with a king-size ego and a bird brain. This time I want to be sure."

"Oh my dear aunt, you will like him."

"I have to find everything about him before I make up my mind. How will we face Jesus Christ?! Isn't this incest? I have been reading about this in 'Sons and Lovers' by DH Lawrence. Very similar to your story."

"What rubbish! Dilip is not my son!"

"He reminds you of your son, he's a reincarnation of your son."

"So be it. This goes to prove that we are soul mates and no one can take us apart."

"Holy Jesus! The Lord has blessed us by taking away your real son, otherwise your relationship with him would have been an embarrassment for us all."

"How dare you talk like this?" Cindy broke down at her aunt's wicked thoughts. She however realised the truth in what her aunt had said.

Gloria immediately went up to her niece and hugged her. "This is a blessing from Jesus, it is a very sacred relationship," she said. Then she kissed her forehead and cheeks. Cindy kissed her back on her cheeks. It was a miracle. She had found the truth she was looking for. They were soul mates indeed.

GETTING TOGETHER

Dilip was in a similar state. Liora was the only person who knew everything about him. He told her about the night before. She looked sad, although there was nothing that she was not aware of and knew what was coming. She told him that it was all because of his mother fixation. He readily accepted this but was not bothered about what others would say. He was helpless, madly in love with Cindy. His only concern was Cindy. What was she going to do next? Liora watched him all the time, he looked tense and utterly restless.

Liora decided to change his mood by taking him out for a movie. They went to the nearest cinema hall to watch a Hindi film. She just sat there holding his hands and watching him all the time. He looked preoccupied till one scene in the movie upset him. Liora noticed his face go red when he heard the hero say, *"Chhaati thok kar usne kahaa, aa jao saamne, sab ke sab, maine apni ma ka doodh piya hai.*" (He thumped his chest with his fist and said, come on, all of you together, I have the strength to take you on because I was breastfed by my mother.)

Liora was quick to realise this. She got up and said, "I don't like the movie, let's go to Victoria Memorial and sit on the lawns there. He got up and followed her. Victoria Memorial was crowded that day. Some vendors were selling cheena baadam (peanuts) while others offered moshla moodi (spiced rice puff) or chana jor garam *(spiced roasted chickpeas)*, singing, "*Babu main laaya mazedaar chana jor garam. (Sir, I have brought lip-smacking spiced roasted chickpeas)*" People were sitting in groups munching cheena baadam with jhal noon (salt and red pepper). Kids were running around, kicking a ball.

Dilip and Liora were not in a mood for all that and they decided to head back home. Liora stretched herself on the sofa with her head on Dilip's lap. Dilip started massaging her head with his warm and loving hands as he always did. This gave him a lot of peace and Liora enjoyed it immensely.

Suddenly, the telephone started to ring and Liora rushed to answer it. A moment later she called out to Dilip who was surprised to know that the call was for him. It was Cindy calling from Gloria's house. She sounded excited and Dilip's hands started to shake in nervousness. He was thrilled to know about Cindy's meeting with her aunt. Cindy was going to take a tram from Ballygunge to her house in Park Street and she asked Dilip to come there. Dilip in Park Circus was almost midway. If he timed it well, he could board the tram she was in when it crossed Park Circus.

Liora could see the transformation in Dilip after the conversation. He had a spring in his step now. She was relieved too, her love for him was causeless. She and her entire family were indebted to Dilip in many ways.

He was getting ready to leave. "It is too early to go, Dilip. Calm down, it will take her at least ten minutes to walk to the Ballygaunge tram stop and the tram takes 30 minutes to get here. If you leave now, you will be waiting for her for 35 minutes."

Dilip knew Liora was right. He smiled in acknowledgment and Liora took his hand in hers. Was this a brother-sister relationship they were not aware of? They began to walk hand in hand in silence before Liora gave him the signal to leave for the nearby tram stop. Dilip walked with long strides to reach the stop quickly and then seeing the tram at a distance, ran to it. He got inside the first compartment where they usually sat. She was not there. He was disappointed. Was she in the earlier tram? He then saw the next tram at a distance and Cindy was there looking lovely in her pleated dark grey skirt and a sexy pink top. He boarded the tram and they hugged each other, hardly conscious of the people around.

PURE LOVE TRIUMPHS

This was pure love. She was his strength. He worked to be worthy of her and this made him successful and prosperous. He was able to bring all the Anglo-Indians together. He helped them with the formalities for their migration to England, Australia and Canada. This was all due to Cindy's influence on him. He even helped Bert. As a result, Cindy and he were made the chief guests at the party Bert hosted a week before leaving for Perth. Bert and his friends heaped praise on Dilip and this was a high point in Cindy's life.

Cindy too flourished beyond Gloria's imagination. Gloria wrote an article in 'The Statesman' about Cindy's achievements. This motivated Cindy who took pride in keeping herself younger, fitter and sexier than before.

Everything was falling into place but the migration plans of Liora's family seemed to have stalled. They had been struggling to migrate to Israel since 1948. Her father had been seriously ill and bed-ridden. Now that he had recovered, the migration papers he managed were no longer valid. Dilip used his political contacts and one morning his contact came over with some good news. *"Dilipda! Hoye gache kaaj ta hoye gache. David ke bole dao! (Okay Dilipda, your work is done. Tell David it's all done.)"* Dilip was thrilled. He ran to meet Liora who kissed him profusely.

The scene at Dumdum airport was emotional. Liora and family were leaving for Jerusalem. It was not easy for Liora and Dilip to part after 16 years of being together. Just before security clearance, Liora broke down, ran up to Dilip and hugged him tightly. He too was very emotional and he kissed her. Her mouth lost control and took control of his. They were lip-locked for a long time and as she parted, tears flowed freely before giving way to a pure smile that gave Dilip all the solace he needed. What kind of love was this? She knew him more then he knew himself. He was overly protective of her since childhood, how could she go away from his life all at once? He had no idea how Liora felt, when Cindy suddenly came into his life. He had vanished from Liora's life into a world of his own. She was so understanding, so caring, was this sisterly love? No, she wanted him in every sense and yet loved him for what he loved and who he loved. Now, he understood what Cindy meant when she said that love was impossible to define.

Cindy was sad that she had had virtually no interaction with Liora. She and Liora had not met and yet they knew a lot about each other. Dilip was a common factor and they both threatened to complain about him to the other. This common agenda resulted in respect for each other.

As the weeks went by, Cindy and Dilip began to spend more time together. They were, however, in each other's thoughts all the time. This was the source of their energies. They were held in high regard by both, Indians and Anglo-Indians. Was this God's way of saying that he loved the most, the ones who love?

A truly blessed twosome!